For Vanessa. Sorry about all the slugs.

–S. S.

Published by
PEACHTREE PUBLISHING COMPANY INC.
1700 Chattahoochee Avenue
Atlanta, Georgia 30318-2112
PeachtreeBooks.com

Text and illustrations © 2023 by Sandra Salsbury

Edited by Kathy Landwehr
Design and composition by Adela Pons

The illustrations were rendered in watercolor.

Printed and bound in March 2023 at at R.R. Donnelley, Dongguan, China.
10 9 8 7 6 5 4 3 2 1
First Edition
ISBN: 978-1-68263-482-0

Library of Congress Cataloging-in-Publication Data

Names: Salsbury. Sandra. author. illustrator.
Title: Spreckle's snack surprise / Sandra Salsbury.
Description: First edition. I Atlanta : Peachtree. [2023] I Audience: Ages 4-8. I Audience: Grades K-1. I Summary:
"A celebration of found family. experimentation. disappointment. and delightful surprises. plus what's truly important in life–delicious snacks."– Provided by the publisher.
Identifiers: LCCN 2022056201 I ISBN 9781682634820 (hardcover) I ISBN 9781682635148 (ebook)
Subjects: LCSH: Dragons-Juvenile fiction. I Chickens-Juvenile fiction. I Domestic animals-Juvenile fiction. I Families-Juvenile fiction. I Snack foods-Juvenile fiction. I Humorous stories. I CYAC: Dragons-Fiction. I Chickens-Fiction. I Domestic animals-Fiction. I Families-Fiction. I Snack foods-Fiction. I Humorous stories. I LCGFT: Picture books. I Humorous fiction.
Classification: LCC PZ7.1.S2537 Sp 2023 I DDC 813.6 [E]-dc23/eng/20221206
LC record available at https://lccn.loc.gov/2022056201

SPRECKLE'S SNACK SURPRISE

SANDRA SALSBURY

PEACHTREE
ATLANTA

Spreckle was hatched on a farm.

She had a fluffy mama,

brothers and sisters

everywhere,

and a cozy bed.

It was a fine home, except . . .

. . . the snacks were not very good.

SLIMY
SLUG

In fact, the snacks were becoming a real problem for Spreckle.

And Spreckle was becoming a real problem for everyone else.

Naturally, Spreckle thought that a life without a decent snack was hardly a life at all. So she did what any reasonable creature would do.

Spreckle flew the coop.

TOO POKEY

The outside world was full of so many snacks.

Spreckle decided to try them all.

TOO DARK

THE SANDWICH FARM

TOO GRASSY

TOO GOOPY

While those snacks may have been good for other animals, they were not good enough for Spreckle.

MAYBE?

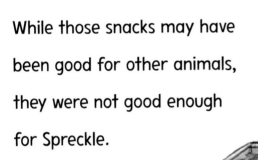

TOO MUDDY

She wanted the *perfect* snack.

Thankfully, she had the perfect idea.

Really. She thought of it
all on her own.

Now this snack wasn't any
ordinary snack, like a a slug
found under a rock or a bucket
of dried corn.

EXCITING
COLOR!

SURPRISING
TEMPERATURE!

SHINY
TASTE!

BUILT-IN
HANDLE!

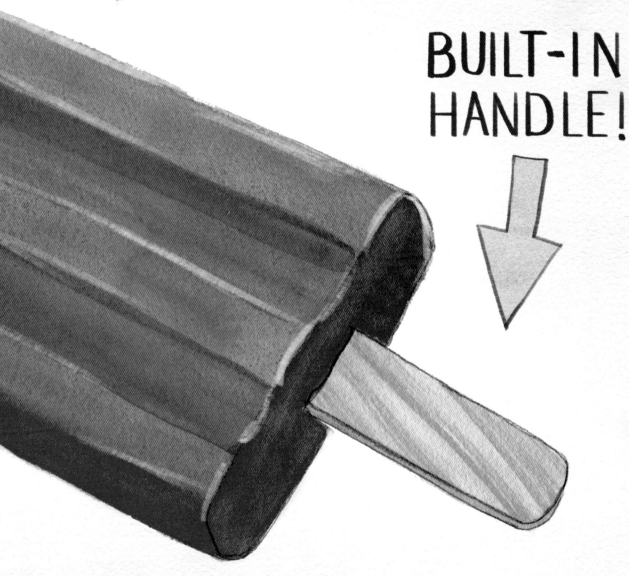

It was a fancy snack.

But unfortunately for Spreckle,

the perfect snack was a lot harder to catch than a slug.

It disappeared a lot faster than
a bucket of dried corn.

A *lot* faster.

And believe it or not,

it was also messier than slugs.

Whoever said this was the perfect snack
must have had a serious case
of brain freeze.

Obviously, there were no good snacks anywhere in the entire world, so Spreckle had no choice but to **never eat anything ever again.**

Spreckle did not need that fancy snack.

Spreckle did not need any snacks.

Spreckle did not need anything at all.

Yes, Spreckle thought the farm was a fine home indeed.
And maybe, if shared with the right company, even
an ordinary handful of dried corn could be . . .

STILL
TOO ICKY

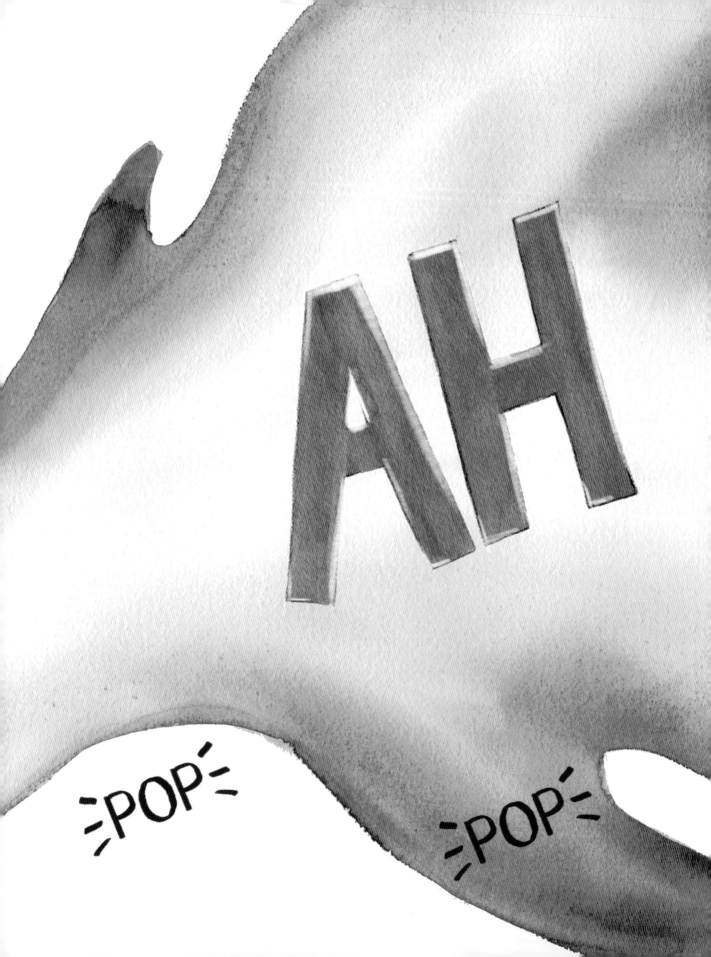

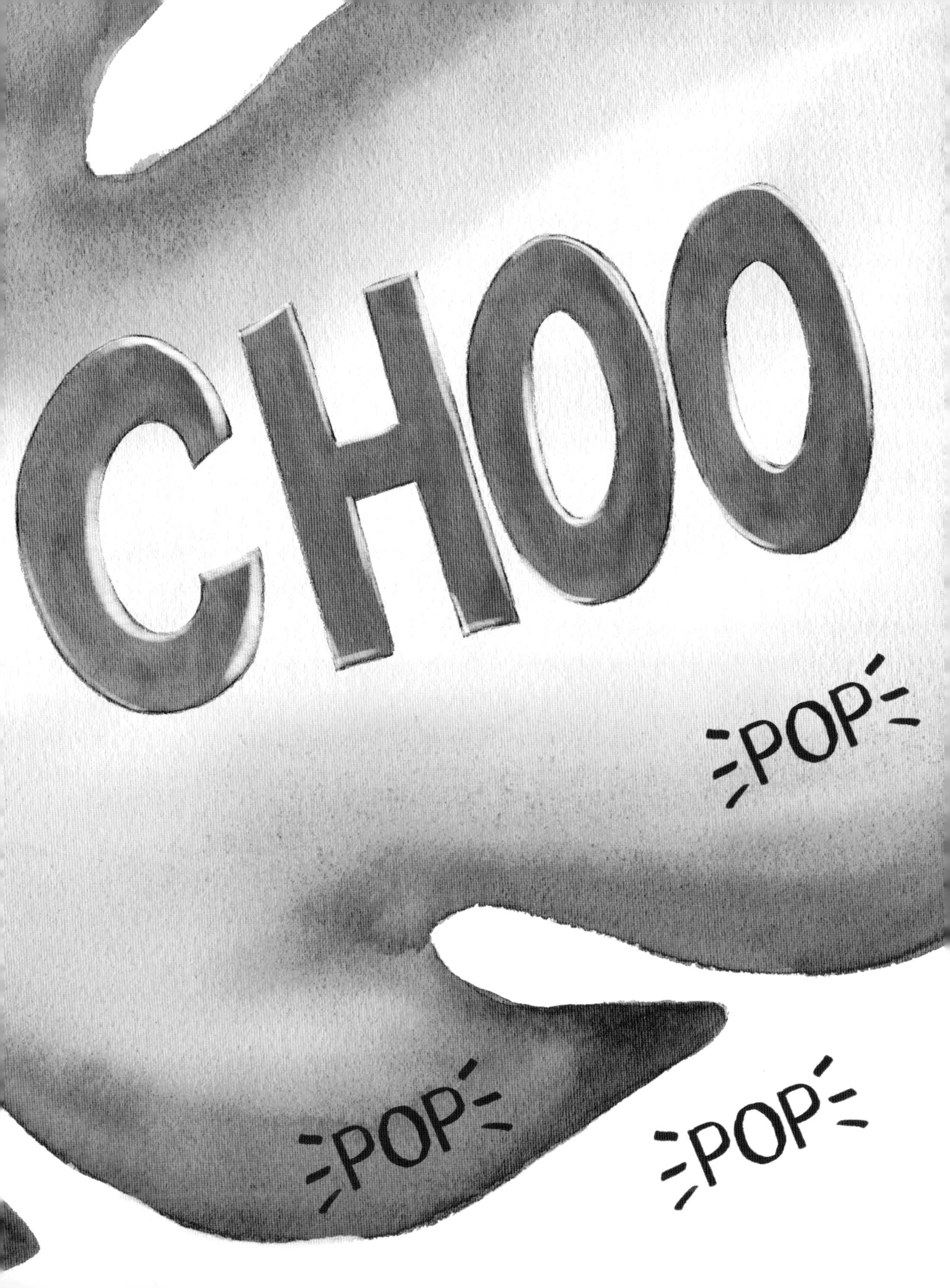
CHOO
POP
POP
POP

The perfect snack!

FLUFFY!

CRUNCHY!

DELICIOUS!

POPCORN!

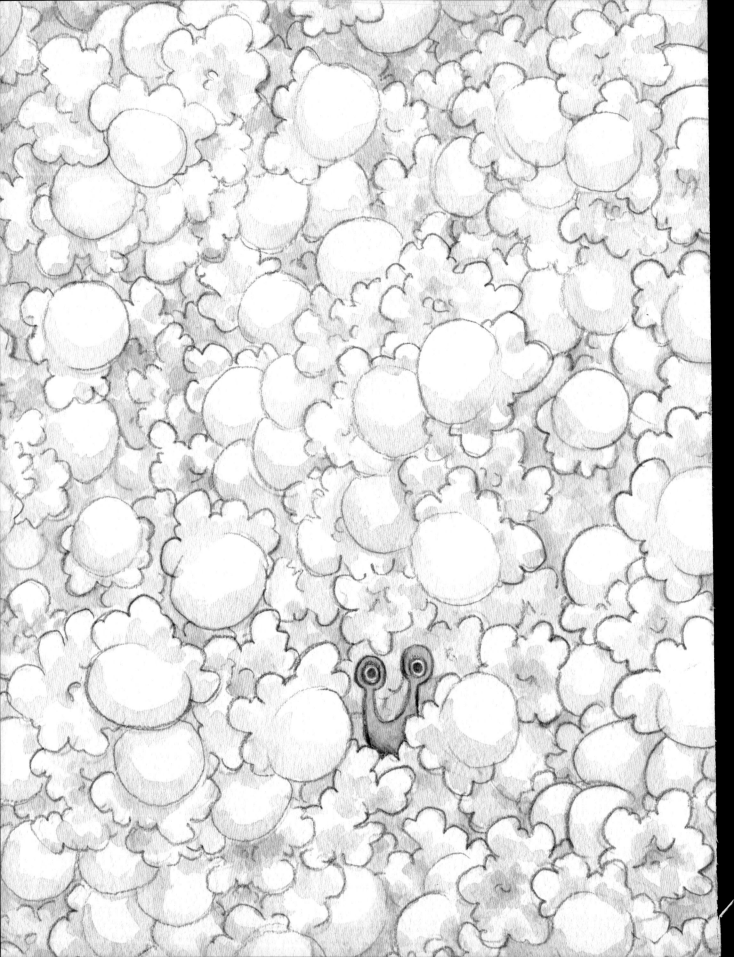